Witch Bazooza

Dennis Nolan

Prentice-Hall, Inc.
Englewood Cliffs, New Jersey

Printed in the United States of America   J

Prentice-Hall International, Inc., London
Prentice-Hall of Australia, Pty. Ltd., North Sydney
Prentice-Hall of Canada, Ltd., Toronto
Prentice-Hall of India Private Ltd., New Delhi
Prentice-Hall of Japan, Inc., Tokyo
Prentice-Hall of Southeast Asia Pte. Ltd., Singapore
Whitehall Books Limited, Wellington, New Zealand

10   9   8   7   6   5   4   3   2   1

Library of Congress Cataloging in Publication Data

Nolan, Dennis.
Witch Bazooza.

SUMMARY: Witch Bazooza wants to win the prize for
having the scariest house on Halloween, but her spells
don't quite turn out as she expects.
[1.   Halloween–Fiction.   2.   Witches–Fiction]
I.   Title.
PZ7.N678Wit   [E]   79-12715
ISBN 0-13-961573-3

It was the morning before Halloween. The wind howled and blew leaves about the old house on the hill. Lightning flashed and a candle flickered in the tower. Witch Bazooza had risen early and gone to the tower with her cat Ajax.

She spent over an hour searching through old trunks and boxes when she suddenly held up a large dusty book.

"Here it is, Ajax," she cried, "Advanced Spells and Incantations for the Serious Witch".

She sat down and began reading the chapters called "Decorating your Home for Halloween" and "Haunting with a Personal Touch".

"I just know we can win the contest, Ajax," she said. "These are going to be the spookiest decorations ever. The Witches Judging Society will just have to give us first prize for having the scariest house."

When she finished reading, she went downstairs
to the living room.

"Are you ready, Ajax?" she said. "Let's start with
the windows." Witch Bazooza raised her wand,
wrinkled up her face, closed her eyes and chanted.

"Sounds unheard, words unspoken,
May the windows in this house be broken!"

Every window in the house shattered at the
magical command! Witch Bazooza looked about
the room and smiled. Then she wrinkled up her
face, closed her eyes again, and chanted a second
time.

"Rusty hinges, and squeaky doors,
And then I want some creaky floors!"

She ran around the house making sure all the doors squeaked, and she jumped up and down to test out the floors.

"Oh, this is just wonderful," she cried, "Simply marvelous."

Ajax purred in agreement.

"Now I think the corners need a little something."

"Witch's hat, and witch's broom,
I want cobwebs in every room!"

"Oh, yes! And a couple of spiders," she added.

"Well, now it's beginning to look like Halloween," she said, as a big black spider ran up the wall.

As she walked up the long winding stairway, she said, "Let's fix up the tower."

She entered the room and chanted once again.

"Fuzzy little bats, with leathery wings,
An owl that hoots and a ghost that sings!"

Suddenly the room was alive with the sounds of moaning and who-whooing and the fluttering of bat wings.

"Oh dear, I almost forgot," she said, and whirled
about chanting once more.

"I've got an owl that hoots, and a ghost that
    moans,

Now I need a skeleton with clanky bones!"

Witch Bazooza and Ajax went back to the living
room as the skeleton rattled and banged about.

"Now for the final touch," she said, as she moved a table up to the front window.

"I need my centerpiece here, so everyone can see it when they come trick or treating tonight."

Once more she wrinkled up her face and closed her eyes.

"To finish decorating this old place,
I need a pumpkin with a jack-o-lantern face!"

"Hurry Ajax," she said, as she rushed out the door. "It should be growing out in the garden!"

The garden was mostly bramble bushes and old gnarled roses with a few stick weeds and mushrooms. Only one plant looked fresh and green.

"There Ajax!" said the witch pointing at the bright green vine. They ran to the plant, but found that the pumpkin for which Witch Bazooza had chanted, was only a cucumber with a jack-o-lantern face.

"Oh, drat! Something must have gone wrong. I'll chant once more."

"No-No-No, hear this sound.
A jack-o-lantern must be around!"

With that, a big bright red beet burst out of the ground. It also had a scary jack-o-lantern face.

Witch Bazooza began to scream and fret, and loudly chanted once more.

"This thing's wrong, it's all red,
Orange is the color of a pumpkin head!"

A second later, a fat orange carrot popped out of the ground!

Witch Bazooza stamped her feet on the ground and screamed.

"Magic broom, and witch's hat,
A jack-o-lantern must be fat!!"

A vine popped out of the ground and began
growing. Witch Bazooza and Ajax followed it,
watching it sprout leaves and finally flowers.

"This is it, I just know it," said Witch Bazooza
anxiously.

But the vegetable that grew on the end of the
vine was a watermelon.

Now Witch Bazooza became wild! She was determined to get that pumpkin. She tried every spell she knew. Soon her garden was over-run with corn jack-o-lanterns, zucchini jack-o-lanterns, tomato jack-o-lanterns, potato jack-o-lanterns, lettuce, strawberry and even rutabaga jack-o-lanterns. Witch Bazooza finally flopped down, tired and depressed.

"Well, we sure won't win first prize now," she
said.

"Look at my garden, what a mess! And I still
don't have a pumpkin. What good is a haunted
house on Halloween without a pumpkin?"

"Come along," said Witch Bazooza, walking
back to the house, "We might as well eat dinner.
No trick-or-treaters are going to come to a house
without a jack-o-lantern in the window."

Halloween Night came and Witch Bazooza's house howled with the sounds of the Ghost. Skeleton bones clanked as the wind whistled through the broken windows. The floors creaked as Ajax paced around the room. Witch Bazooza sat quietly, watching the bats flutter about.

Just then, she heard a knock at the front door. She raced down the steps from the tower room, across the creaky floors and pulled open the squeaky door.

"Trick-or-treat," said a tiny voice. It was Melissa, the little girl who lived down the street. She was dressed as an angel. Witch Bazooza looked around to see if there was anyone with her.

"The other kids said it was too scary here, with the jack-o-lanterns all over your yard," said Melissa, "So I came alone."

Witch Bazooza stepped out onto the porch. Candles lit up each of the vegetables and their scary grinning faces glowed in the dark night.

"My goodness, it does look rather spooky, doesn't it?" said Witch Bazooza.

"It sure does," trembled Melissa.

Witch Bazooza dropped a candy spider into Melissa's bag and wished her a Happy Halloween. She closed the door and went back to her room.

"You know, Ajax?" she said, looking out the window, "This place looks pretty scary, even without a pumpkin."

At midnight, Witch Bazooza was startled by another knock on her door.

"Now who could that be?" she said.

She peeked out and there stood Head Witch Karessa Bonza, Witch Hepzabah and Witch Abadaba from the Witches Judging Society.

"Come in," said Witch Bazooza.

"Allow me to present you with the first place trophy," said Head Witch Karessa Bonza. "I also wish to congratulate you on your wonderful new decorating idea. Every other house had the standard pumpkin jack-o-lantern in their window. Your garden full of faces was so original and unique that we decided to award you the first prize."

"This is for you," she said, handing Witch Bazooza the trophy. It was a gold pumpkin-shaped
cup with a jack-o-lantern face.

"And that's not all," added Witch Hepzabah. "As a bonus, your house will be haunted by Sir Reginald Archyduke's ghost for an entire year!"

"He's the one who clanks his chains and rattles his armor," said Witch Abadaba.

"Oh, thank you so much," said Witch Bazooza. "This is the Happiest Halloween ever."

The witches hopped on their brooms and flew off into the night. Witch Bazooza and Ajax watched them go, then took one last look at the garden, and closed the door.

The sudden sound of clanking chains and rat-
tling armor made Ajax's fur stand up straight.
"Oh, silly cat!" laughed Witch Bazooza. "That's
just Sir Reginald Archyduke's ghost."

Witch Bazooza walked across the creaky floor of the living room and placed the trophy cup on the mantle.

"Just look, Ajax," she said, "We've got a pumpkin after all."

That night, a very happy Witch Bazooza and Ajax slept quite soundly, while Sir Reginald Archyduke's ghost clanked and rattled with all his might.